I0822420

KRISTOPHER JEROME

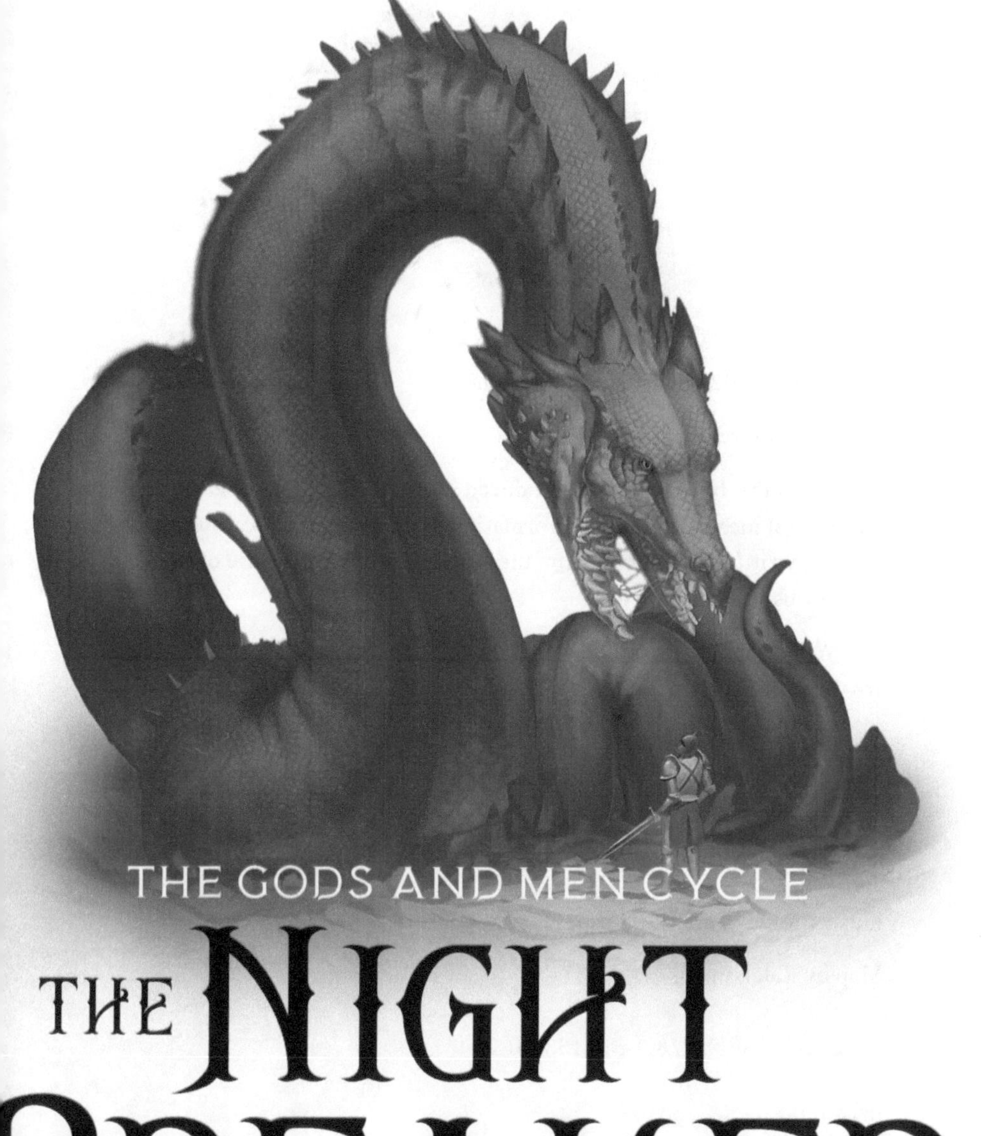

THE GODS AND MEN CYCLE

THE NIGHT BREAKER

A PRELUDE TO
SUNDERED FROM HEAVEN

Cover art by Milica Celikovic

Cover design by Miblart

Illustration by Patrick Buermeyer

Map by Ralarismaps

Hardcover ISBN: 978-1-951138-20-2

First Edition, June 2017

Dark Tidings Press LLC

PO Box 593

Albany, OR 97321

darktidingspress.com

ALSO FROM DARK TIDINGS PRESS

THE GODS AND MEN CYCLE

By Kristopher Jerome

The Broken Pact Trilogy:

- Wrath of the Fallen
- Cries of the Forsaken
- Tears of the Godless

The Nightbreaker

White Wings from Grey Ash

Before the Breaking:

- A Bandit's Balance
- A Voice from the Darkness
- In the Shadow of Light
- The Sons of Lighthammer
- The Bard's Demons
- Disciples of the First Cycle
- Ten of Seatown
- The Last Gift of Kane Darksend
- The Grey God's Edict
- The Blood-Soaked Sacrament*

*Forthcoming

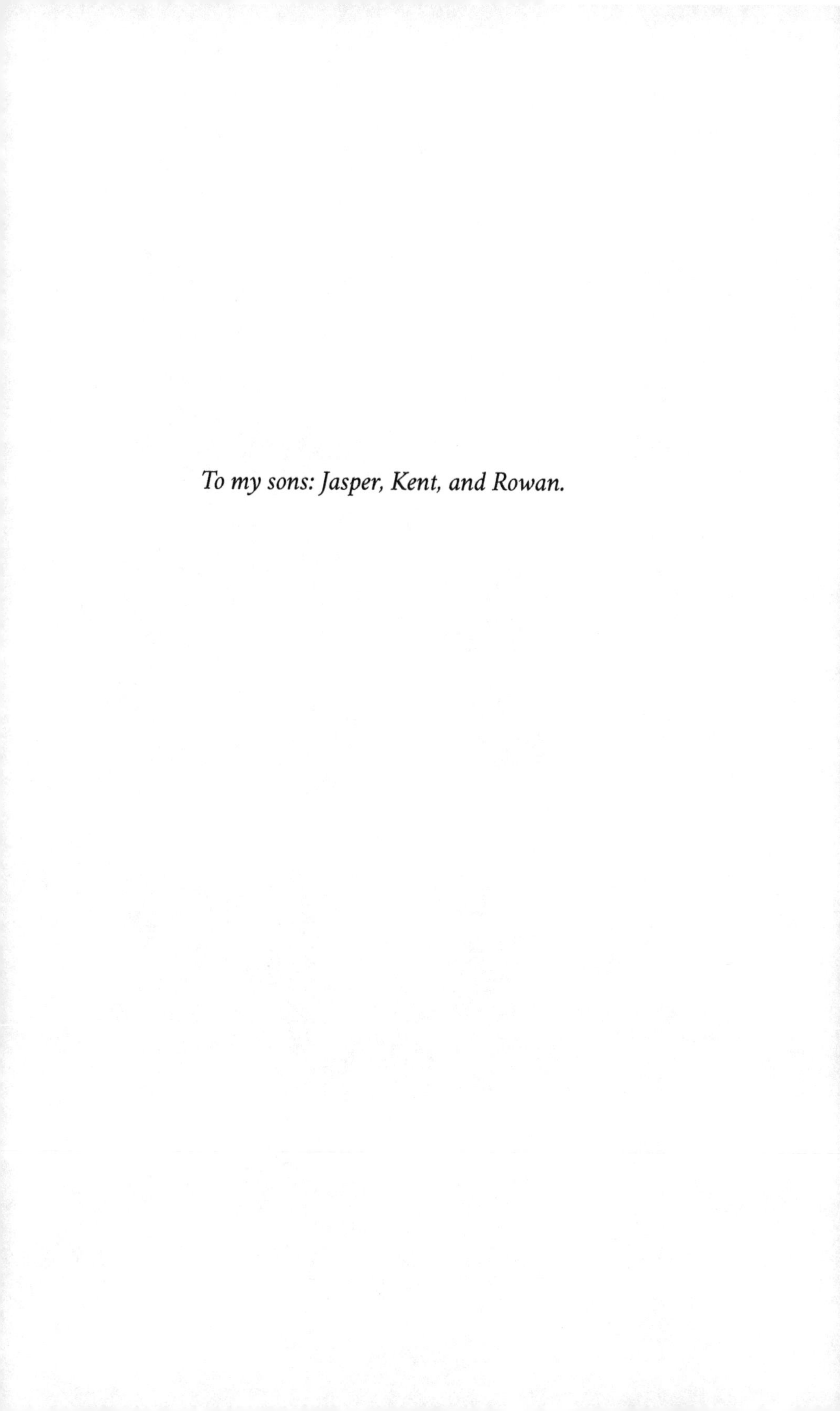

To my sons: Jasper, Kent, and Rowan.

Artorus
The Rim of Paradise
Illux
The Nameless Sea
The High God's Tears

THE NIGHTBREAKER

1

123 AC

The dust of the plains caked his face and clogged his nose. Sunshine glinted off of the armor of his companions and blinded him, but still he and the others kept on the hunt. They had no choice but to do so, or else their enemies would escape and they would be seen as failures. It didn't matter how small or unimportant any individual task was—the safety of Illux relied equally upon them all. The winged Seraphs glided past him on either side, brandishing swords and axes both. Blue energy crackled in the air about the fliers. What he would give to have the Divine Blood as they did. But Daniel was merely a Paladin, a fact that his commanders never let him forget.

The heat from the sun overhead was maddening in his armor, causing sweat to pool inside his plate mail and make his smallclothes stick to his skin. They hunted a pack of Demons far to the southwest of Illux, far from any settlement or outpost. Illux had wished to send only Seraphs on this hunt, but Lio had insisted that some of the Paladins accompany them as well. Not all of them could bear the Divine Blood, he would say, but all of them could bear the burden of this war. None could argue with the words of a god, not even the Seraph High Command.

It wouldn't be long before they caught their quarry and returned to the walls and farmlands of the city. Fatigue had finally begun to set in as Daniel's boots thundered onto the dusty stone. His breaths were short gasps, and his muscles burned. They had tracked these Demons for days: a band of no more than twenty that had ambushed and killed a group of travelers foolish enough to leave the safety of the city. Most did not attempt the dangers of the wilderness for this very reason. Demons prowled all of the unclaimed places of creation. Now that Daniel and the others had almost caught sight of the monsters, the chase had truly begun.

Daniel looked at his cohorts, a group of some ten Seraphs and thirty Paladins. The Paladins were men and women like himself, broad and armored in white steel. They had been imbued with the divine energy of the Gods of Light, giving them a strength that no regular mortal could hope to achieve. Few of the other Paladins looked as tired as he felt, a fact that they wouldn't hesitate to remind him, for they continually looked for reasons to tell him that he was inferior. Daniel was the product of an evil act. A child of sin.

The Seraphs that flew above and beside him showed no signs of the weariness that the Paladins felt, eternally energized by the silver blood of the gods that flowed through their veins. Each was held aloft by great white wings that carried them effortlessly on the winds. They were a sight to behold, even for an experienced Paladin such as Daniel.

Ahead of the small force the dusty stone carried on

endlessly into the horizon, rising and falling with the hills beneath it. Few ever travelled this far south for the lands were unmapped. How far the High God's creation truly extended none could say. The creatures of the Gods of Darkness usually occupied these areas in force, but the fighting in the north seemed to have pulled most of them away from here. Suddenly, a cry rose up from one of the Seraphs, Asmov, who flew at Daniel's left. He was pointing far ahead where the familiar glint of black armor caught the sun.

Finally, they had them.

Just then, a dark shape cut through the air, knocking the Seraphs from the edges of Daniel's vision. Abruptly, the charging stopped as the confused warriors on the ground gathered together, brandishing their swords and scanning the skies. None had thought to look for danger from above. They had been told that there were no Heralds with this band of Demons. They had also been told that none of the Divine Beasts had been seen in this area of late. Hopefully *that* intel wasn't wrong as well. Daniel crouched lower to ground as he scanned the area.

Then, seeing a flash of red light, Daniel dove to the ground and rolled to the right as a ball of fire split the earth and disrupted his thoughts. His ears were ringing, throwing all of the cries and screams around him into a muted cacophony. One of the men next to him was soundlessly screaming and clutching at the melted ruins of his face. Dizzily, Daniel pulled himself to his feet, trying to ignore the sight of the other man. Daniel saw that his screaming companion had less flesh than bone left upon his head, with what little was left of his eyes staining the top of his breastplate. The man was clearly beyond healing, so Daniel gave him the mercy of a quick sword-stroke to the neck before gazing south.

The Demons came on in unison, each running at a break-neck pace in the direction of the now scattered Paladins. The Seraphs were returning now, barking orders as they flew past. At their lead was Asmov, the hooked-nosed messenger casting a wary glance at Daniel and his now bloodied blade. His eyes flashed over Daniel and onto the man at his feet.

"Fan out!" he cried as he whizzed past, his wingbeats sounding like the pounding of a drum in Daniel's still weakened ears. "The Heralds won't stay down for long; we must deal with these Demons, and quickly!"

They did as he commanded, each of the Paladins spreading apart and making their way toward the onrushing Demons. Daniel noticed that not all of the Seraphs had returned with Asmov. Already this attack was becoming more than they had bargained for. If they had known Heralds were present, perhaps Lio would have sent more Seraphs.

Is our revenge really worth more loss of life?

He did not relish the fighting as others did; yet he fought as if he were born for it. In moments he was in the thick of the Demons, twisting and turning to avoid their wicked sword-strokes. It was not more than another few short moments before the red blood of Daniel's fallen companion that covered his blade was replaced with ichor that ran black. The Paladin squared off with one of the beasts, taking his attack to the Demon before it did the same to him. Daniel's sword cut deep between the onyx plate of his foe, finding its mark before the creature had a chance to defend itself from him. He pulled free the blade and raised his hand. Blue energy sprang to life between his fingertips and hammered the dark shape back into the mass of its fellows.

The Paladins swarmed the Demons like a shining silver tide, pressing their advantage of numbers where they could. In the sky above winged shapes flitted back and forth, sending showers of silver and black blood raining below whenever they met one another. It appeared that the Heralds had returned to the fray. Daniel felt the heat of Demon-fire wash over him from the left and right as he was pelted with small stones that burnt his skin. All about him was the chaos of battle and bloodshed.

A Demon's sword bit into Daniel's shoulder, bringing him back to reality. The dark, serrated blade sliced through even more steel and skin as it was pulled free. The pain gripped hold of him, rendering his left arm nearly useless. He could waste no time healing in such a battle, so he pulled his arm close to his body and tried to ignore the throbbing warmth than ran down the length of it. Daniel lowered himself into a crouch and prepared to spring at his foe when a crumpled form from above landed between them. White wings were splayed out at odd angles. A puddle of silver and red blood began to pool underneath the carcass.

It was the Demon who sprang first, jumping over the fallen Seraph while Daniel was still frozen in place. The Paladin had allowed for the creature to take advantage of a momentary lapse in focus, and he would now pay the ultimate price—unless he did something, and quickly. Daniel jumped to the left, keeping his weakened side away from his foe. His arm still hung, uselessly, at his side. The Demon landed where Daniel had been just moments before. Both of their swords met. They struggled against each other until finally the Demon gained the upper hand and pushed

Daniel back a step. He could feel the crusted surface of the plain cracking underneath his feet. The Demon pressed its advantage, pushing the desperate Paladin back farther and farther.

Just like Daniel wanted.

Daniel had only been giving the struggle the smallest amount of his concentration, focusing instead on the shredded flesh of his arm. Earlier he had thought that there would be no time to heal himself, but now he made the time. All he needed to do was heal his arm just enough that it was useable again. The warming magic seeped into his bones, mending the damage done by his enemy. The bleeding subsided and most of the muscle and some of the flesh above knitted back into place.

He rolled to his side as the brute swung again, its sword striking empty dirt. Both of Daniel's hands firmly gripped his blade. He struck the creature across the knee. Ichor and metal, each black as pitch, erupted from the wound. The Demon collapsed to its right while it struggled to remain standing. Then Daniel's sword removed the thing's head in one stroke. Nearly exhausted, he dropped to his knees and looked around at the carnage surrounding him. Most of the Demons had fallen, as had many of the Paladins. Smoke filled the air in many places, creating a haze of blue and grey. A scarlet muck made of blood and ash covered the ground on which they fought. Overhead, Asmov and his remaining Seraph companion had finally dispatched the last Herald, which plummeted earthward, a smoldering husk.

It's over. Was it worth it?

The two Seraph's landed near Daniel, yet they seemed to ignore him. A thin layer of soot had blackened the wings of the two warriors. The Paladins on the outer fringes of the battlefield made their way in toward the commanders, some nursing wicked looking wounds. Asmov barked an order to his companion who then took a quick headcount.

"We have lost nearly half sir," he said. "Briant, Jenny, Re—"

"Enough!" Asmov cut him short. "It matters not. They have rejoined the High God. Let us go."

After he spoke his eyes fell on Daniel. The scorn in those bitter orbs told the Paladin what he already knew. Hate like that was unmistakable, and rarely hidden. His commander had never liked him. The Seraph hated being the caretaker of a product of sin. Yet, even he had superiors, and they had commanded him to treat Daniel as he would any other. Too bad, then, that even with Divine Blood, he was only human.

"I am glad that the sacrifice of the fallen holds so much meaning to you," Daniel said as he stood.

The Seraph walked closer so that he could address this insubordination quietly. Daniel noticed that Asmov gripped his sword far tighter than he should have now that all of their enemies were gone. His scowl was so fierce that for an instant Daniel regretted having spoken up. The crisp white hair of the Seraph was plastered across his face. As he got closer it was clear that it was stained with blood both red and black. From a distance that now seemed to be widening, the other Paladins watched in a quiet curiosity. None of them would speak on Daniel's behalf, even if he hadn't been a sinspawn.

"What did you say to me, *Unclean?*" Asmov asked through gritted teeth.

"I said nothing to offend, sir. It is good that you care so little," Daniel retorted. "We have little time for emotions like sadness or gratitude toward those we have lost."

A hand that was surprisingly strong gripped Daniel by his throat and lifted him off of his feet. He struggled to breathe, while trying desperately to hide as much of his discomfort as was possible. The lines that crossed Asmov's face finally began to blur as Daniel's vision darkened.

"I don't know why the gods have tolerated you thus far," Asmov spat. "You, who were born of rape. The Gods of Darkness put their mark on you in the womb. I, however, will not tolerate insubordination from my men, no matter who commands me otherwise. Speak to me in such a manner again and I will cut out your tongue."

Daniel dropped to the ground in a heap and lay there gasping for longer than he would have liked. The air that he desperately forced into his body burned his throat and lungs. His hatred burned far hotter than even that. There would come a day when he would no longer be punished for the sin of his father, a day when he would stand up to men such as Asmov. But today he would settle for just breathing. Small stones were scattered about the ground that he lay upon. They dug into his skin and cut his face, all the while feeling as if they were vibrating faintly. Tears began to well up in the corners of his eyes. He tried to hold them back, but a rumbling from below shook them free.

Something is below us...

"Move!" Daniel shouted as he jumped into the air.

Just then, the very earth on which they all stood heaved outward. Men and bodies went flying in every direction while the sky darkened above them. Daniel lifted upward with the thing that came from beneath, his body soaring up as if he was a Seraph. Then he felt himself falling farther than should have been possible. When he landed his head struck a stone, letting the rushing blood break free of his scalp. The earth under him rumbled again, but this time it was not from the movement of something below its surface, but from the roar of something towering above it.

He opened his eyes and gazed up in horror through the limited light at the thing that now beset them—a force of nature made flesh. A Divine Beast. They had been told that all such creatures were in the conflict to the north where they did battle with the gods and each other. This one took a shape that he did not recognize, so perhaps it was something new?

The creature was hard to make out in its entirety, for the sky behind it had somehow darkened as if it were night; not even Aenna, the ever-present and always-glowing opening to the Divine Plane could be seen. What he could see, dimly outlined, was long and limbless, like some giant snake or worm. It roared again, its jaw splitting apart like mandibles as it did so.

Daniel pushed himself back to his feet. Beside him, Asmov was unconscious. The snake-creature thankfully looked away from the pair, choosing instead to slither further out of the earth to follow several screaming Paladins who ran in the opposite direction. Its girth was so large that even while it moved on the surface it shook the ground beneath their feet. Few of the Divine Beasts were quite this large, and those that were inspired fear in even the gods that created them.

Daniel knew that there was no way they could defeat such a being without more aid. Their only chance would be to run as far from the beast as possible, and pray to the gods that it did not follow. He looked at Asmov one final time before turning and running toward the safety of the horizon.

Distant screams greeted his ears as the Divine Beast began to feed on his companions. Men and women cried out in pain and fear as their lives were snuffed out, one by one. The Paladin stopped running and listened for a moment. They would all die if he didn't do something. Those were the same men and women who scorned him and hated him. But they were also his brothers and sisters. What kind of a man was he if he did nothing?

The same kind of a man that they claim I am.

Daniel spun about and made his way through the darkness toward the sounds of death. Retracing his steps, Daniel found himself back at the side of the fallen Seraph. Bending low he placed his hands upon Asmov, feeding him just enough healing energy to restore him to consciousness. The eyes of the fallen commander slowly fluttered open, staring at the darkened sky in disbelief.

"What happened? How long have I been out?" he asked slowly.

"Not long. This thing darkens the sky somehow," Daniel replied. "Get up. While you still have men left to command."

Asmov stood and tried to gaze through the darkness at the shadowy outline of the creature slithering across the plains. Suddenly, small flashes of blue light illuminated the monstrous thing as it chased and devoured the handful of fleeing Paladins. Even with a blue tint lighting the beast here and there, its flesh seemed to emit darkness. A solitary winged figure flew about the creature, lashing out with godly fire at its head.

"Dex," Asmov said. "The fool. The thing will kill him."

It seemed that the Seraph was right, for the attacks of his winged subordinate seemed to be having no effect on the great being ahead of them. His barrage of blue flame was doing little besides giving the killing ground some limited illumination that was gone almost as quickly as it appeared. As it was, the Divine Beast seemed to hardly even notice the gnat that buzzed so desperately in its ear.

"Quickly, we must join the others," Asmov commanded.

"Wait," Daniel said, grabbing his arm.

The Seraph spun on him, the shadows of his face dimly lit by the distant flashes of blue light. His visage was contorted into a snarl of rage so pronounced that it seemed to make him more akin to the Demons that they had been fighting earlier than the Paladins that they now rushed to save.

"Don't you dare command me! What is the meaning of this? Be you a coward as well as the product of sin?"

Daniel tried not to shrink back as he spoke, keeping his voice as level as he was able. "I am no coward, but we cannot blindly rush in just to join our fellows in death. Dex isn't even drawing the notice of the thing, and that is the key. If you two can find a way to distract it I can lead the others to safety."

"Safety?" Asmov asked. "Where would that be?"

"There," Daniel pointed pointed back the direction from which they had come. "It doesn't matter where we go, but how far. If you two can distract it long enough for us to get farther away than it is able to sense us, we should be safe."

"Move then!" Asmov shouted.

The Seraph turned and began flying through the darkness toward the source of the flashes of light. Daniel sprinted after him, leaving his sword lying in the dirt behind them. Little good a blade would do for him against a thing like this.

The creature had chased the survivors of his band farther than he had initially realized. Asmov disappeared ahead of him moments after he left, hidden even from the distant illumination caused by Dex. The darkness seemed to stretch on before him forever, interrupted only by the occasional flashes of blue light. Daniel had to focus so as to not stumble across the rough terrain as he followed blindly behind where the Seraph must have been. Finally, he could just make out Asmov reaching the side of Dex and adding his own fire attacks to those of the lesser Seraph.

Daniel began to stumble now, as he got closer to his quarry. The slithering of the great beast may not have been as fast as the Paladin could run, but the way it shook the earth as it moved made running all but impossible. Still, he stumbled on, sometimes blindly, sometimes led by the flashes of light. Finally, he was near enough to the front of the beast that he could clearly make out the outline of his remaining companions. There were only three left.

Hurry up Asmov. Find a weak spot.

Like an answer to his prayer the creature stopped slithering forward and roared in agony. It writhed about, shaking the ground to the point that Daniel collapsed to his hands and knees. It was with great difficulty that Daniel was able to look skyward and see what had happened to the thing. The Divine Beast lifted itself into the air, swinging its head about to try and catch the small fliers that harried its head. Daniel pulled himself up again and got the attention of the other Paladins.

Then the creature spoke, and all thoughts of escape dissipated.

"Do you think that you can escape by blinding me?" it bellowed. "I am Rexin the Blasted. I do not need eyes to see you. I only need rock and earth."

With that pronouncement it was plunging earthward and the ground again erupted in a shower of stones and dust. Before Daniel knew what had happened the thing was beneath them all and the earthquakes were receding. There was no time to wait and see if it intended to return.

"This way!" he shouted.

The few haggard survivors turned and followed him back the way that they had come, hoping desperately for the safety that the horizon promised.

It was not to be so.

The ground began to shake again, more furiously this time than it had the last. The earth all around them began to heave while the Paladins each cried out. Daniel felt the end come upon him even though he couldn't see it.

Then the ground was far below him.

Daniel looked down in shock as the earth was again torn open and the great beast called Rexin the Blasted was lifting itself above the surface. It was then that he finally noticed the hands that firmly gripped him under his arms. Dex and Asmov must have swooped in to save who they could. He could hear the Paladin who had not been so fortunate for a brief moment before he was tossed into the gullet of Rexin. Mercifully, Daniel could only just make out the shape of the beast, so he didn't see his sister-in-arms lose her life.

Flying over the beast was the vague outline of another Seraph and a Paladin. Daniel knew that this other Seraph must have been Asmov. The grizzled commander would never have been the one to save Daniel. In the darkness it was hard to make out any details beyond the shape of the two warriors. Suddenly, the Seraph dipped too low, from stupidity or exhaustion Daniel couldn't tell—either way it came at the wrong time. The great snake lifted itself higher out of its tunnel and swung wide, catching both figures in its open maw.

Daniel looked away toward the blackness ahead. He hated Asmov, but he would have wished such a fate on no man. Dex didn't seem to be having the same trouble carrying Daniel to safety, even though he had expended more energy attacking the

Divine Beast than Asmov had. The sounds from behind seemed to indicate that the creature had returned below ground. After a long while of flying through the darkness the sun returned to the sky as if nothing had been wrong, a final indicator that they were no longer being hunted.

Finally, Daniel looked over his shoulder at his savior. It was Asmov. Daniel nearly cried out in shock. Had the Seraph known who it was that he had saved in the darkness? If Asmov was surprised he showed no signs of it, remaining sullen and silent.

So it was that the two bitter enemies flew back toward the salvation of the City of Light and away from the darkness of the plains.

2

It was cold at the latrine trench behind the fort; far colder than it should have been. Daniel shivered, shook, and headed back to the small stone arch that marked the entrance to his prison. The moonlight lit his path through the short scrub grasses that pressed up against the protective wall and through the archway into the courtyard. The little tower loomed over the stone walls that encircled it, men and women walking their circumference. Daniel supposed that it would be his turn for wall duty soon. Little that it mattered to him, anyway. If he wasn't walking the wall he would be sitting atop the tower looking out into the blackness. He preferred the solitude to the card games and carousing taking place within the tower.

He had been stationed here for months, ever since Asmov and he had returned to Illux from the incident on the plains. The campaign in the north was still where he wanted to go, where what few friends he had left had gone, but he had been left behind. Merek had bidden Daniel farewell just before Daniel had gone on the mission to the plains, and his other friends had left while he was away. And now he was here, at the edge of the known world, pissing in a hole in the ground. This had to be Asmov's doing. When the two had returned to the city they had been scorned—the survivors of a failed mission and the bearers of dire news. There was sometimes no crueler fate than being the messenger.

They had stumbled upon a new threat to the champions of the Light. Rexin the Blasted, as it styled itself, was a Divine Beast of a magnitude rarely witnessed. Even Akklor the Unbidden paled in comparison to this creature. Its ability to blot out the sun and tunnel beneath the earth made it an enemy that even an army would struggle to suppress. What little remained in Illux of the Seraph High Command had deemed the beast beyond their means to dispatch and, therefore, low on their list of priorities at this time. Even the Gods of Light chose to focus on more pressing matters. As such, the warnings of Daniel and Asmov were ignored and the outcast Paladin was given this post as payment for sins that he did not commit. What had become of Asmov he did not know. Being a Seraph gave him extra privilege and honor, most likely sparing him a post such as Siltstone Tower.

The bastard is probably leading some force in the Rim right now.

Daniel stopped just short of the tower door, his hand resting upon the iron handle. Inside Rooker and Fiora would be playing a hand of cards no doubt, or some other game of chance. He could join them if he wished, but he didn't think that he could stand the icy stares or quiet snickers this night. Neither did he have luck enough for such games anyway. Instead he turned and made his way up the small stair to the wall, waving at Bast who simply shrugged as he walked past and headed for the tower. Bast was short for a Paladin, but the young warrior seemed no less hardy than the others. He did tend to keep any negative remarks about Daniel's heritage to himself, which had caused Daniel to prefer his presence to that of the others, in any case.

The night sky was clear; only small wisps of cloud hovered in front of the moon. Beside the white disc, Aenna glowed faintly. Daniel was sure that the High God must have been peering down through the window in the heavens at the sinner who disappointed him. From his vantage point on the wall Daniel could see far to the hills in either direction, dark shapes that were illuminated by the silver light from above. Trees dotted the hills in small clusters, the distant edges of a larger forest.

This outpost sat at the edge of the land under the dominion of Illux, as far from the white walls of the great city as any men dared settle. They were to the southeast, only a few days ride from a large body of water, if the maps were to be believed. Few had ever traveled to the shores of that place and returned to speak of it. Divine Beasts were said to patrol those waters in far greater numbers than they did on land, fighting their own proxy war without the clusters of mortal armies to hinder them.

Outposts like this served as an early warning system for the city in case the armies of the Gods of Darkness made their way toward Illux from the wilderness beyond, where they gathered en masse. It was an outpost such as this one that had first seen the dark shapes of the enemy descending from the Rim that had started the northern campaign.

As such, it was unlikely that there was any purpose to this

post at the ass-end of the Mortal Plane. All of their enemies were far away to the north.

Adding to the illumination of moonlight, the light of small torches yellowed the walkway atop the wall every few yards. But it was the gulfs of silver night between them that made Daniel feel more comfort as he passed through them. He felt that less of his soul could be seen in the moonlight, less of the blackness inside. His mother had never told him the nature of his conception; that had come from the mouths of those around him as he'd grown. He had faced shame from children and old crones alike as a boy. His father, whatever kind of man he had been, had taken his mother by force one night, leaving her with child. Like all other sinners, Daniel's father had been banished from the city walls, cursed to walk the Mortal Plane as a servant of Darkness, doomed to become a mindless Accursed that served Demon masters. For all Daniel knew, he had slain the man in the intervening years since he had become a Paladin.

Even though the crime was no fault of Daniel's, nor that of his mother, it was said that he was born of Darkness. Therefore, it was assumed that, deep down, he must be a servant of Darkness.

A wind blew across his face, waking him from his dark dreams. Below, the door to the tower opened and closed as Bast went inside, allowing the sounds of laughter to drift out for a brief moment before they were silenced by the click of the latch. The card-players always gambled and joked into the late hours of the morning, sleeping just before their shift to watch the wall. Others still slept above them in the upper reaches of the tower, somehow undisturbed by the noises from below. At any given time at least two Paladins were on watch for any signs of the enemy, patrolling the circular wall that surrounded the courtyard at the base of the tower. If Demons or Accursed were seen, there was a signal pyre at the top of the tower that could be seen for miles in every direction once it was lit.

Prayers would be said if that fire was ignited, prayers that would alert the gods quicker than any flame. But prayers were often missed, buried in the deluge of such pleas that filled the mind of the Gods of Light at any given moment. Before the war moved to the north, each of these towers held a Seraph who would simply communicate with his or her god to spread the word of an attack. Recently, none who held the Divine Blood could be wasted on such remote areas.

Yet we could waste them hunting Demons in the wilderness.

Rooker stumbled out of the doorway, cutting the courtyard with a shaft of gold. No doubt he was headed for the latrine before finally catching some shut eye before his inevitable watch. Rooker's path meandered this way and that, his drunken shambling drawing Daniel's eye. The fool wasn't headed for the outer gate, but instead made his way slowly up the stair to the landing above. When he was at the top he leaned over the edge and emptied his bladder over the wall.

The idiot is liable to fall. I wouldn't mind.

Even so, Daniel made his way toward the drunk, on the off chance that he would be needed to prevent a tumble into the darkness. Across the way, the other watcher continued her rounds, ignoring any possibility for an accident. Rooker wasn't as popular as he would have assumed, then.

Daniel reached Rooker just as the man finished his business and swung about, leaning on a nearby parapet for support. The torchlight gave a grim cast to his slackened features by the time his eyes fell on Daniel.

"What'd you want's, you s-stupid sinspawn?" he slurred.

"Just watching that you don't fall, you fool," Daniel shot back.

Rooker looked confused for a moment before turning and shambling back down the steps. Even drunk he should have been able to return the way that he had come safely by the light of the moon and the torches. Daniel didn't feel the need to escort him any farther, so he let the drunk go alone. Suddenly, the moon was darkened and a wind blew so hard that some of the torches flickered and died. Rooker tripped over his own feet in the newly-minted darkness, falling the rest of the way down to the base of the tower. His cries of pain were cut off by the panicked whinnies of the horses that were stabled within the courtyard.

The night seemed thick—denser than Daniel would have expected from a few torches blowing out. He instinctively looked to the sky, hoping that he would see a large cloud covering the moon. There were no clouds that he could see. Neither was there light of any kind.

"Gods have mercy," Daniel whispered.

The Paladin tore one of the last remaining torches from its fastening on the wall and bounded down the steps toward his fallen companion, his mind racing through all of the possibilities that now faced them. There had been no clouds in the sky earlier this night, no signs of a storm. Even if there had been, Aenna, at least, would still be visible. The unnatural darkness that assaulted them could only mean one thing. Fear gripped him, fear like he hadn't known since he was a boy. There was no escaping this thing twice. Finally, he reached Rooker, the drunken Paladin nursing a bloody wound to his temple. Perhaps the fall had been fortuitous, for it seemed to be sobering him up some.

"What in the High God's name happened?" he breathed. "Where did all of the light go?"

Daniel helped the man to his feet as he answered him, "I've seen this once before, months ago in the plains to the south. We must tell the others. We are about to be attacked by a Divine—"

The ground shook furiously, sending both men back to their knees. Somewhere to Daniel's right he heard a sharp cry as the other watcher fell to the ground below. The fact that the woman was most likely dead meant little as Daniel fought to regain his footing. There were far more lives that would be snuffed out in the coming moments. The horses were so fearful that they fought against the wooden barrier that kept them enclosed. Fiora threw open the door to the tower just as the ground beyond the wall erupted into a shower of debris. A large, snake-like shadow slithered above the wall, towering over them like an adder above mice.

We must get away from the ground.

Without speaking, Daniel grabbed Rooker by the arm and pulled him into the open doorway, pushing Fiora back into the tower and closing the door behind them. Rooker drunkenly stumbled into Bast, who disgustedly pushed the other Paladin aside. Daniel pointed up to the higher levels of the tower as the sounds of the horses' whinnies turned to human-like shrieks of pain and fear. The Paladins bounded up the steps to the floors above, forcing any who stood in their way to turn back. Some tried to speak or cry out, but Daniel silenced them all with glares or hands clamped over mouths. He knew that it was a long shot, but he hoped that if the creature could not feel or hear them it would think that they had fled the tower the moment it had arrived. Just as before on the plains, they had no hope of defeating it without more help.

They finally reached the uppermost level, all dozen or so of the Paladins quietly panting. The floor still shook slightly, but the movement of the creature seemed to have lessened or gotten more distant. It seemed that Daniel might have, at the very least, bought them more time. None dared move within sight of the small windows that were cut into the stone around them. No one knew just how good the vision of this thing would be. Outside, the horses had all been silenced, leaving nothing but sounds of wind whistling through the courtyard below. A small hatch in the ceiling led to the signal fire. More than one pair of eyes darted up at the opening. Duty required them to light the beacon and hopefully spread the word of the attack, but doing so would surely damn the Paladins in the tower to a quick death. Daniel knew that he was likely not alone when he took the time to pray to whichever god would listen, but none of them had any way of knowing if such a task had been successful.

What if the creature isn't even heading for Illux? We could be lighting the flame for no reason.

It did seem strange that a creature such as this would waste the time making itself known to one of the outposts. If it truly meant to attack the city all it had to do was tunnel there, and none would be the wiser until it was too late. Perhaps they had just been unlucky, like the last time he had run into the beast? Or could it be that this thing was clearing the way for some larger force to attack Illux while the bulk of the army and the gods were in the north?

Daniel knew that he couldn't sit idly by and put the city in danger any more than he could knowingly condemn those who sat beside him to die. They had all sworn an oath to give their lives for the city, an oath that none of them had taken lightly, and yet…

Mustering his courage, he crouched below one of the windows and peered out into the blackness beyond, hoping to gain some sight of the giant thing. Far below, the light of the last few torches looked like the small stars that had dotted the sky before the creature had arrived. Once his eyes had adjusted, he could make out the shattered remnants of a large portion of the wall, along with the enclosure that had housed the horses. Of Rexin the Blasted there was no sign.

Daniel turned and looked back at his companions, the relief on his face surely visible, even in the blackness.

Then the tower groaned, followed by a thunderous crack. Stone slid upon stone as the floor began to careen slightly beneath him, causing what few furnishings that adorned the room to slide toward the wall. Daniel stumbled into Rooker, sending the other Paladin out the open window, tumbling to what could have been his death if not for the hand that gripped his ankle. A giant of a Paladin, a man called Springjack, supported himself next to Daniel, holding onto Rooker as he screamed and flailed about. Bast came up beside the pair and gripped Rooker by the same leg that Daniel had held onto. Quickly, the three men pulled Rooker into the building and returned him to the tilted floor. The drunken Paladin seemed to have completely sobered from the experience, yet he still emptied the contents of his stomach onto the ground.

The tower groaned loudly again as the stones began to grate on one another. Still, it seemed as if the imminent collapse of the tower had stalled for the moment, the ancient masonry withstanding whatever was poised against it. All around Daniel, his fellow Paladins were beginning to shows signs of panic. Each of them was struggling to keep upright and slow the inevitable slide into the eastern wall. Again the opening to the signal fire above caught his eye. Perhaps lighting the signal would be a waste of time, but it gave them one last obstacle to overcome before they all died, one last victory to strive for. Springing to his feet, the determined warrior pulled himself up through the opening and onto the roof of the tower. In the center of the flat rooftop was a massive pile of dried brush and a few small barrels filled with tree pitch. A small lean-to covered the majority of the pile from the elements, lest the wood get too wet to ignite.

Realizing that he had brought no torch, Daniel called back down the opening. Grumbles of dissent greeted his ears, but a few moments later the light of a torch passed through the opening and and into his outstretched hand. The flickering light illuminated the worried face of Bast as he handed the probable cause of their demise to Daniel. Daniel tossed the torch into the brush pile, lighting the signal in an instant. The hungry flames rose and greeted the unnatural darkness, a candle in a cavernous room.

Now they had to hope that the next closest tower would see that fire and ignite the next beacon in the sequence. The darkness that engulfed Siltstone tower was cut by the light of the roaring fire, as was the beast that encircled it.

Daniel saw that the creature known as Rexin the Blasted wrapped around the great tower like a snake squeezing the life from a fresh kill. Rexin seemed to notice the fire almost belatedly, swinging its great head upward to gaze upon the defiant light that crowned the tower. The Divine Beast lifted itself up above the top of the flames, an orange glow dancing upon its wicked face. The creature seemed larger than Daniel had remembered, perhaps a trick of the light, or simply the fact that he could actually see the monster clearly now. The eye which faced him was milky white, and the flesh around it bubbled and blackened, rather than the golden brown of the rest of the creature's face.

Asmov did wound you, beast. You are not invincible.

Its head swung about and gazed on him with its good eye. It roared then, a deafening sound that made the tower beneath him groan again as its grip tightened. Rancid spittle from within the mouth of the creature sizzled as it landed among the flames. Daniel pulled free his sword and shouted back at the beast, refusing to back down from its challenge.

"I know you, creature!" he shouted over its roar. "You didn't kill me on the plains, and you won't kill me now!"

Then it dove, open-mawed and roaring again while Daniel slipped back down into the hole and dropped to the floor beneath.

"With me!" Daniel yelled. "We must get below!"

The others followed him back down the stairs as the ceiling above collapsed in a shower of stone and flame. The creature was roaring loudly again, this time in pain as the flames from the signal fire erupted over its body, the barrels of pitch covering it in a wreath of fire. Smoking globules of flaming pitch filled the raw opening at the top of the tower where the Paladins had been huddled just moments before. The stones around them seemed to sigh in relief as the monster's grip loosened for a moment while the fleeing Paladins stumbled over each other on their way down the steps. Ahead of Daniel, Bast reached the closed door, blasting it open with a flash of blue energy from his outstretched fist. Just as he stumbled into the darkness beyond, the tower cracked again and quickly fell in on itself. Daniel pushed the rest of his companions through the open doorway before falling out onto the shaking earth. Plumes of silt and smoke erupted from behind them, covering the survivors in a thick coat of dust.

The fallen Paladin pulled himself to his feet and led the others through the breach in the wall, away from the crumbling tower as quickly as they could run. Behind them, the tower had completely collapsed, leaving no signs of the structure or its flame in the darkness. Fiora stopped running to look back over her shoulder, only moving again once Daniel firmly pushed her to keep her going. There would be no safety behind them now.

It seemed that Rexin would not follow them this night, but Daniel knew that he had not seen the last of the Divine Beast.

Nor have you seen the last of me.

3

"It's about time," Rooker coughed as the walls of Illux rose before them on the horizon.

How many days it had been since they had escaped the creature, none could say. Fiora had been keeping track at first, but she'd quickly tired of the affair and returned to a grudging silence. It had been many more days than it should have been, in any case. The Paladins were not making the progress that their greater stamina would have normally allowed, eschewing speed for a safer and more methodical approach back to the sacred city. Daniel walked at the front of the group, his hand constantly resting upon his sword and his eyes scouring the horizon behind them for any signs that they were being followed. At night he found that he could barely sleep, instead he constantly caught himself listening to the ground for any rumbles or vibrations. Mercifully, the skies had remained relatively cloudless on the journey back to Illux, letting the moonlight wash over the landscape and sparing them the heart-pounding horror that absolute darkness would have brought.

He had thought that the others would have mocked him for his overly-cautious behaviors, but they had refrained. Until they reached the gates of Illux at least, it seemed that he had been entrusted with the role of keeping them alive. In other circumstances, it likely would have been Fiora or Bast that would have been the natural leaders of the band, but for some reason Daniel had filled that role from the moment he had lit the beacon.

The forced march that they had embarked upon had been at a more frantic pace at first, fear of Rexin's return urging them onward, even through the circuitous route that Daniel had made them take. Weariness had overtaken them quickly, though, and weariness always wins out over fear. Now, with the city walls just within reach, Daniel finally allowed himself to admit that they had escaped the death that had come so near.

Even so, he knew that they marched away from one danger and toward another.

"Do you think anyone will even believe us?" Fiora asked, squatting down to rest.

"They must, if we have any hope of overcoming that thing," Daniel responded.

"What about that Seraph you mentioned from the last time?" Rooker asked. "The one who's a prick?"

He spat after that last remark. Seraphs weren't respected by all members of the Paladin order.

Nor will they ever be if more of them wield their power like Asmov...

"Surely all of the city won't have gone daft," Bast interjected. "I still have friends in high places I can call upon if need be."

"We shall see," Daniel said sullenly, motioning for the others to end their rest and follow him once more.

He still couldn't believe that it had been Asmov who had pulled him to safety at the last moment those months before. The two had barely spoken since their escape, and Daniel didn't relish the idea of possibly coming up against Asmov or any of his ilk again. The last time he had returned to the City of Light after a failed encounter with the beast had not been a favorable experience. The more he thought about his temporary banishment the more he was sure that Asmov had somehow focused more of the blame for the failed mission onto Daniel's shoulders. It wasn't hard for a sinspawn to become the scapegoat for the failings of those around him.

This time would be different, though. He knew that it would. This time he had multiple allies at his back, possibly for the first time in his life. Even Merek couldn't stop other citizens of Illux from looking down on Daniel, not by himself, no matter how hard he had tried.

The small group wandered along the path that served as the road to the southern wilderness, slowly picking their way past abandoned carts and dropped belongings. No human corpses littered the area where Daniel could see them, although the bones of more than one horse poked up from between the human-caused refuse. Most of these objects hadn't been touched by human hands for months or even years. From time to time the City of Light would find itself besieged by the Forces of Darkness. That made little time for those who were outside the walls to make their way in before the end came.

If I keep walking back like this, I will know this road better than my old neighborhood in Illux.

Few lived outside the walls of the city, none wishing to

abandon the safety of the gods for the wilds beyond. After all, was not the ultimate punishment for sin banishment from the golden gates? Even so, a farming community would sprout up here and there, hopeful that the gaze of the Gods of Darkness would never fall upon them. Those who willingly fled the City of Light often did so to escape the stifling rules of Illux, to escape the judgments laid upon sinners. The banished far outnumbered the willful departures, though, for those who committed crimes against their fellow man were still common in this late day.

The man who raped my mother.

Daniel brushed what little emotion he still felt for that man out of his mind. His mother had raised him to be better than that.

Ahead, a dark shape darted under the shade of an overturned cart. Small eyes gleamed out at Daniel before a stone cast by Rooker sent the thing back into the shadows. It had likely been a scavenger of some kind, picking at the horse bones or some rotten food left behind in one of the carts.

Fiora cast the old drunk a stern glance but he paid her no heed. Rooker hadn't been himself since they had fled the crumbling tower, but then again he hadn't had a drop to drink since then either. Save for perhaps Bast, the pair had become Daniel's staunchest supporters, and it had been these two who had possibly hated him the most before.

"What are we gonna do once we get there?" Rooker asked again, rubbing the stubble on his chin.

Daniel swallowed hard. The truth was that he didn't know.

"I will demand an audience with the gods," he said somewhat meekly.

"Last I heard, they were all up north," Fiora replied.

"Not all of them," Bast said. "Illux can never stand alone. One of them will be there, and they will want to know what happened."

"Whichever god that may be," Daniel began, "I will make them understand the danger that we face."

He couldn't tell them that he was planning on going back the way they came, if the gods allowed it. Chances were that they suspected that already. The real question would be whether or not they would follow him in his folly. Alone or with an army of thousands, Daniel would march back down this very road and finish that beast.

Damn, I would rather be up north.

The walls rose ever higher, their white brilliance reflecting the distant rays of the sun. The golden gates hung open, as they did at all times from sunrise until sunset. Daniel supposed that the traffic coming and going from the city while the northern campaign raged on would undoubtedly be low enough that they didn't need to be kept open, but some traditions were upheld even in the face of common sense. The gates would have a guard posted, but otherwise there was no real need to fear—the gates could be closed quickly enough that no enemy force would be able to threaten the city and farmlands inside the walls.

Once the ragged band was near enough to the southern gate, they saw a small group of men on horseback ride out to greet them. Their number was large enough that they kicked up a sizable plume of dust in their wake. This seemed odd to Daniel. It wasn't often that any from within the city greeted what few travelers there were unless they were a war party of note. When the horsemen neared, they brought their mounts to a halt and gazed menacingly at Daniel and his companions.

The leader, a brown-skinned Seraph, removed the helm from her head before she spoke, allowing her braided hair to fall between her shoulders.

"Who are you and why do you approach the southern gate?" she asked.

"We are survivors from an attack on one of the southern outposts. Siltstone Tower," Daniel said.

"An attack?" she asked. "We heard of no beacons lit. Were you cowards that deserted your post?"

It was then that Springjack shoved forward, pushing aside Daniel and Bast. The large warrior's war hammer was already in front of him, a clear sign of his displeasure at the remark. Springjack was a mute, his throat partially removed by a Demon's blade some years before. He gestured emphatically with the hammer, first at Daniel, then at the Seraph.

The Seraph and all of her companions drew steel.

"What Springjack here meant to say," Rooker began as he drew his own sword. "Is that we don't take kindly to being called cowards."

Daniel quickly stepped between the two groups, holding up his hands. The horses began to nicker and dig at the earth while the Paladins at Daniel's back all pulled forth weapons and tried to crowd around him. This was not at all starting how he had hoped.

"We did not desert. I lit the beacon myself," he said.

"Are you the commander of these?" the woman asked him sharply.

That comment was met with barely concealed snickers from the men at her back. She looked over her shoulder slightly confused until one of her companions leaned in and whispered in her ear. When she looked back at Daniel she regarded him even more coolly than she had before. He had been recognized by one of the men at least, it seemed.

"Sinspawn," she murmured under her breath.

"We were attacked by a Divine Beast called Rexin the Blasted," Daniel said, ignoring the insult. "It was the same creature that slaughtered the expedition south under the command of the Seraph Asmov. Is he stationed in the city?"

She seemed to have looked past him now, peering at the armed men and women at his back instead.

"Sheath your steel under the command of Tyga, Commander of the City Watch of Illux, on pain of death. You are all prisoners until we sort this out."

The group looked around questioningly but began to lower their weapons. All but Springjack, who stood completely in front of Daniel now.

"I demand an audience with Gods of Light," Daniel said, forcing the woman to lock eyes with him.

Tyga laughed. "Samson, Luna, and Arra are leading the campaign in the north. Only Lio sits in the cathedral this day, and I doubt he will speak with the likes of you, *sinspawn*."

Before Daniel knew what had happened, Springjack had used his hammer to topple Tyga from her horse, the animal rearing and falling onto its rider moments after. It was chaos then. The other riders lifted their swords and rode in a tight circle, hacking down at the cluster of Paladins with an unexpected savagery. Thankfully, the Paladins hadn't waited to react. Flashes of blue and streaks of silver burst into existence as magic and steel was brought to bear. Bast jumped onto one of the horses, sending its rider into the mob below where he was quickly set upon by Rooker. Fiora hammered at where Tyga lay with magic, keeping the Seraph from rising. Springjack silently swung his great hammer in a circle, keeping most of the riders at a safe distance.

Lio, help us.

Then Tyga was up suddenly, her face contorted in rage. Her own blade flashed and Springjack was left holding the haft of his hammer in two pieces. She knocked Fiora away with a bolt of white lightning and turned on the mute giant again. The next swing of her sword would have removed his head from his shoulders had Daniel's own blade not stopped Tyga's attack mere inches from Springjack's face. Over his shoulder Daniel heard Rooker curse and Bast cry out in pain.

A white light flashed, blinding him. A gust of wind howled in his ears and the shaking of the earth sent Daniel to his knees. As he lay on the ground, still partially blinded by the flash, he began to feel a warmth wash over him. It was as if all of the blood in his body was being pulled to the surface of skin all at once. He knew what this meant.

"What is the meaning of this?" a deep voice boomed.

His vision finally returned as Daniel sat upright, looking at the one who spoke. A golden figure floated before him, glowing with a radiance that could not have come from this world. The god was armored just as one would expect a Paladin to be, yet his armor reflected the light of the sun in a rainbow of colors. Long white hair framed his face, which itself was golden like that of a sunset. His features were cut as from stone, yet Daniel could see a softness in them.

Tyga pulled herself to her feet an answered. "When questioned, these men became violent and attacked us."

"Silence," Lio said.

If it were possible, the Seraph seemed to shrink, cowering back from the God of Light glowering at her.

"I was speaking to the one who called me," he continued, turning to Daniel.

Daniel numbly pulled himself to his feet, only to drop to his knee and bow. The Gods of Light were no rare sight, but their very presence inspired such awe that there could be no other response fitting for a mortal to take. Rarely had he ever spoken with one directly as he did now, rarely had one ever answered his prayer or spoken to him like this. Lio was more than magnificent, he was...beautiful.

"My lord, I humbly apologize for disturbing you," Daniel began, weakly. "We meant no offense to the commander. My companions overreacted to a perceived slight against me and our honor."

Tyga spat then, the phlegm landing in Daniel's hair.

"I merely called the sinspawn what he was. These men abandoned their post when it came under siege," she sneered.

"Which post?" Lio asked.

"Siltstone Tower," Daniel responded.

The god looked contemplative then, as if he was weighing some great decision. His golden brow furrowed behind the stray locks of white hair. Lio looked over each of the Paladins standing before him, staring into the souls of each in turn before his eyes finally rested on Daniel. The silence as he stared at the Paladin seemed to drag on for hours before the golden figure finally spoke.

"We will discuss this further at the cathedral. I will meet all of you there just before the sun sets. Until then, there shall be no further outbursts." Lio turned then to Tyga, to whom he added, "The next person to use *that* name again, for this man or any other, will rejoin the High God sooner than they ever expected."

Lio lifted into the air, gently floating back to the city as if he was being carried on the wind. When he was no larger than Daniel's fist, the god turned and looked back at the gathering of Paladins before disappearing over the walls of the city. Tyga spread her wings and then closed them angrily, remounting her horse and galloping back through the gates, her companions quickly following. Bast had, by then, dismounted the horse he had commandeered and threw the reigns to beast's rightful rider.

After they left, Daniel exhaled, for what he felt like was the first time. Rooker somehow looked even more sour than before, but appeared to be otherwise unharmed. The others all seemed to be in similar shape, other than Fiora who was in the process of healing a nasty cut across her forearm with the help of Bast. Springjack put his hands on Daniel's shoulders and nodded in gratitude.

"What in the High God's name was that?" Rooker asked, grabbing the mute warrior by the arm.

The larger Paladin simply shrugged and smiled, turning away to help Fiora and Bast with their healing attempt. Rooker and Daniel watched Springjack go, each looking progressively more puzzled than the other. Daniel looked over his companions as they put away their weapons, trying to hold back the shadow of a smile.

"Why did any of you do that?" Daniel asked after a time.

"You're with us now. Or we're with you now, maybe," Rooker responded distantly. "That means nobody, silver blood or not, nobody fucks with you."

"And how did I earn such an honor?"

"You got us out of a rough spot. All of us owe you for that."

"Really," Daniel began. "I didn't do anything out of the ordinary."

"You got me into that tower," Rooker said. "And then you got me out."

Rooker turned and started walking toward the gate, with Daniel and the others quickly following behind him. Ahead, the walls of Illux towered over them, casting a large shadow over the road. The remainder of their walk to Illux continued in silence, yet Daniel couldn't help but eye all of his companions with a newfound respect.

I won't forget this. I promise.

When they reached the gates of the city, the normal regiment of men had been bolstered considerably. No doubt because Tyga had said something. All of the men and women were armed to the teeth as well. Even so, the throngs of City Watchmen spread to allow them to pass through without conflict. The City Watch was made up of Paladins and humans alike, though more of the latter. As Daniel and his group passed between them, some jeered and snickered, one or two even yelling "sinspawn", though undoubtedly less than would have had Lio not threatened Tyga earlier.

Once they were beyond the shadow of the wall, they passed into the stretch of farmland that surrounded the city proper. Rows and rows of crops stretched from the walls to the buildings a few miles distant. Sun-browned farmers didn't stop their work as the ragtag band passed, used to the comings and goings of the Paladins and Seraphs as they were. Most of those in the fields this day were either unusually young or unusually old. It felt empty here with the majority of the population of the city slogging through blood and death in the Rim somewhere.

Eventually, they reached the beginning of the paved stones

that marked the second border of the city. Stone buildings jumped up about them in an orderly fashion, spreading out from the central point of the city upon which the Grand Cathedral was built. Smaller wooden structures had recently begun to crop up just outside the rim of stone, a sign that the population of Illux was finally growing faster than the wars with Demons and the Accursed could quell it. The multi-storied stone houses and shops towered above the Paladins as they walked down the cobbled streets, small still compared to the walls in the distance or the cathedral at the heart of the city.

To his left, Daniel watched as a woman leaned out of a second story window and poured water onto a large hanging garden. His own home before joining the Paladins hadn't been quite so spectacular, but his mother had loved her flowers. She had told him that some of the wildflowers had come from the Rim. His mother had passed some years before, taken by some sickness that even the Seraphs couldn't cure. Daniel had considered seeking an audience with the gods, but his mother had warned him against taking such an action given his... heritage. His entire life had been spent living in the shadow of a man whom he had never even met, a fact that didn't seem like it would be changing any time soon.

When the sun finally started lowering itself toward the horizon, they found themselves in the giant plaza at the center of the city. The plaza was round, and paved with a smooth white stone which was kept cleaner than any of the streets leading to it. Before them, in the very center of the plaza, loomed the Grand Cathedral, a sparkling structure of four lesser spires surrounding a central spire that reached to the clouds above. The central tower was dedicated to the worship of the High God, while each of the lesser spires was dedicated to one of the

Gods of Light. Across the plaza was an immense square structure that served as the barracks for the Paladins stationed within the city. In recent times the building had remained mostly empty. Daniel hadn't stepped foot inside of it for nearly a year.

The Paladins made their way toward the spire dedicated to Lio, where they expected to find the God of Light. Off to the side of the plaza Daniel noticed that the construction of the four statues to the Gods of Light had not slowed, even with the northern campaign taking most of the able-bodied men and women from the city. The statues were being constructed of gold brought in from the Rim so that the likeness of the gods would be nearly identical to the real thing.

As they rounded the cathedral, Daniel saw a large crowd had already gathered around the faintly glowing figure of Lio, who stood towering above them on the steps of the cathedral. The crowd was made up of Paladins, Seraphs, and normal mortals alike, many of whom turned and pointed at the small group that approached them from the south.

What is this?

Fortunately, or unfortunately as it may have been, Daniel found himself again pushed to the forefront of his companions as they approached and forced their way through the crowd toward the steps at the base of the cathedral. None spoke to them as they passed—everyone heeding the warning of the god, it seemed. The silence among the onlookers was almost more deafening than the jeers that Daniel would have expected.

When they passed near the front, Daniel thought that he saw the familiar face of Asmov gazing defiantly back at him.

"Closer," Lio said when they reached the front of the mass.

Daniel alone mounted the steps, to stand uncomfortably

close to the god. From this distance Daniel was able to look Lio over in more detail than he ever had been able to before. He was filled with both awe and uneasiness. The stone-chiseled features of Lio were unnaturally attractive, causing Daniel to feel an uncomfortable stirring in his body. He craved the god in a way that he could not understand, could never have believed was possible.

"Why are all of these people here?" Daniel asked before silently cursing to himself, shocked that he had even thought to question a god.

"Because I think I know what you have to say, and I want them to hear it."

Good enough, I suppose.

Daniel looked at Lio and then turned to the crowd once the god nodded for him to do so. He stared out at the mass of faces below him, some friendly, many not so. Lio stepped down another step so that he was closer to the Paladin.

"This man and those that he commands were accused of abandoning Siltstone Tower without lighting the signal fire. The penalty for which is death. How do you respond?"

Asmov locked eyes with Daniel from below; his expression looked as if he was willing it to be true, as if that would make all of his hatred reasonable.

"We did flee Siltstone Tower, it is true. But not before lighting the signal fire. I lit the flame myself," Daniel responded.

"Then why did we not hear of it?" a man yelled from below. "Why were the other signal fires not lit as well?"

"Because we were attacked by a Divine Beast," Daniel replied.

Gasps rumbled through the crowd. Daniel thought he saw concern flicker across the face of Asmov.

"We were attacked by Rexin the Blasted," Daniel continued. "The same beast that slaughtered our soldiers in the south those months ago, in the same failure that condemned me to Siltstone Tower in the first place. This creature has the power to blot out the sun, moon, stars, and even Aenna, when it emerges from the earth. The light of the tower didn't reach any of the others because it destroyed the tower as we escaped."

The murmurs from below reached a fever pitch now, with arguments breaking out between those who supported Daniel's claims and those who did not. After several minutes of this it almost seemed as if fighting was going to break out between some of the Paladins and the Seraphs. All the while Lio did not speak, nor did his eyes ever leave Daniel. Finally, he clapped his hands and all were silenced.

"Daniel speaks the truth. Long have we feared that such a creature would come into the world. Nor was Siltstone Tower the only fortress to fall to it," Lio intoned, his words floating through the silence like cotton on the wind. "We have lost word from Seastone. The Seraphs I sent to investigate said that the tower looked like it had been leveled by some great beast that burrowed from under the ground. This creature is using the campaign in the north to attack us while we are undefended to the south."

"What should we do?" someone cried out.

Lio looked again to Daniel.

"I wish to lead a group into the wilderness to track and kill the creature, to break the night that it wishes to bring to our people!" Daniel shouted, a tone of command entering his voice.

"What hope do you have?" a familiar voice asked. Asmov, perhaps.

"I have survived its attack twice, I have seen its weakness.

The Seraphs at the command of our first encounter with Rexin were able to permanently injure it by blinding one of its eyes. That will be the way to end the creature."

The looks that Daniel saw now were a mixture of fear and respect. Many, it seemed, were afraid that they would be called upon to follow Daniel into what would surely be their end. Even if it would save the city, certain death was not a prospect that any below would take lightly. How could any man, even a Paladin, hope to overcome such a beast?

He was sure that they were right. How could he possibly hope to succeed? The confidence and bravado that he was trying to put off was largely for show. Lio was watching, after all. Yet Daniel knew that he would not be able to continue his life knowing that he had left this thing unfinished.

"We cannot afford to leave the city undefended, so I will not command anyone to follow this man on the hunt," Lio said. "But, I will ask, who will follow him?"

It wasn't a surprise to Daniel when the only men and women to step forward were the ones whom he had led into the city. Saving them from Rexin had made them loyal to him—loyal enough that they would follow him right back into the maw of the Divine Beast, it seemed. Out of all of them, Rooker seemed the most annoyed by the situation, but Springjack had a firm grip on his shoulder. Beside them, Fiora was putting on a look of confidence, while Bast actually seemed eager.

No Seraphs? How am I going to make this work without some Divine Blood?

Then Asmov stepped forward, standing in the line behind the others, trying his best to blend in, and failing. This must have been his pride at work, fighting to subdue his desire to live. Daniel tried to hide the shock on his face, but he wasn't sure that he was totally successful.

After several moments with no one else joining the others, it seemed that Daniel's band had formed.

"Take this," Lio said, pulling free his sword. "With my blade in hand you have my blessing at your back."

Daniel fell to one knee and reached out his hands, clumsily clutching the sword when the god placed it in his fingers. The contact was exhilarating.

"In the morning," the god said, "go forth in my name."

4

They had been riding south for several days now, all without any semblance of a plan. How could they know where to find the creature? How would they really kill it once they did? Could they return if they failed? Surely these questions were on the minds of those following Daniel, for they were on his. This quest to which he had appointed himself was based on emotions, not logic. What hope did they have against such a creature when so many had fallen before it? Even with a Seraph? Even with a god's sword?

Daniel looked down at the longsword that was strapped to his side. The blade felt heavy in his scabbard, as if it were forged from a metal denser than any steel mortal smiths had access to. Wings adorned the crossguard, and the metal of the blade was almost whiter than the stones of the cathedral. At night, as he stood watch while the others slept, he practiced with it, swinging and thrusting with the weapon as if he had never wielded a sword before. During the day, the others looked at

Lio's sword just as questioningly as he did, no doubt all of them wondering what powers it possessed.

It better do something.

Springjack rode just behind Daniel, as had become his habit. The mute giant rarely allowed the others to get too close, seemingly having appointed himself Daniel's protector. Even Bast, whom Springjack had been eyeing with a sad expression ever since they'd left the city, was kept at least an arm's reach away. Rooker shrugged the behavior off as one of the many personality quirks of the odd little band. Fiora, though—Fiora had other ideas.

"He has the sight, you know," she said, leaning in from Daniel's left.

"So you've told me," Daniel responded distantly.

There were those who, it was rumored, had the sight. Mortals whose Divine Spark was connected to the High God in some way that gave them powerful premonitions of the future —or, as some claimed, whole visions. As far as Daniel knew it had never been proven, and he certainly had his doubts about Fiora's claims. If this ability was something that truly existed, then surely the gods would have found a way to use it to their advantage in tipping the scales of the war. But since they had never done so…

"You don't believe?" she asked. "He told us that you would save us when you first came to the tower."

"That would explain why Rooker and the rest of you treated me like I was diseased."

"That—" she began. "That was our mistake. Still, I wouldn't doubt Springjack's power. He was blessed by the High God."

"What does the High God tell him about me?" Daniel asked, turning to face her.

"The High God doesn't speak to him, but sends him feelings, sometimes dreams. All that Springjack will say is that you are going to do great things, that you will be the cause of many important events, and that we must all keep you safe."

Suddenly an idea struck him, even as crazy as it may have seemed.

Daniel slowed his horse and turned it about, facing the party behind him. There were no more than twenty of them, but he felt that he now knew each of them better than he had ever known another group of people. The other riders eyed him expectantly, all except Asmov. The crooked-nosed Seraph continued to glower silently, as he had since they had left the city.

Don't you judge me, you hateful bastard.

"I know what you are thinking," Daniel began.

"Do you?" Rooker slurred, the ale skin clutched in his hand. "Cause I don't think I wanted anyone to see that mental image but me."

Daniel ignored him and continued, "There is no way to be sure where this thing will show up again. For all we know it could be behind us, heading for the city already. I have decided that our best chance will be to return to Siltstone Tower and see what signs the beast may have left behind that we can track."

Let's see how powerful this sight of Springjack's really is.

Everyone nodded in agreement, except for Asmov, who turned his horse toward the east and Siltstone Tower. Bast cut the Seraph off, stopping him from continuing until Daniel had spurred his horse to overtake them and return to the head of the party. Overhead, the sun beat down from beside Aenna, uncaring and heedless of the mortals beneath it.

. . .

It was the next day, in the mid-afternoon, when they rode into the still-smoking ruins of Siltstone Tower. The tower was now nothing more than a pile of smoldering stones. Carrion birds encircled the site, some descending to pick at the few rotted horse carcasses that remained. Most of the walls that encircled the tower still stood, but gaping holes split them at various points. The smell of smoke still clung to the place as if the remains of the tower were rotted flesh giving off the stench of decay.

Daniel rode through a breach in the wall first, gently urging on his mount when something about the place kept the animal from going forward on its own. Just inside the wall was a giant pit, seemingly bottomless from where Daniel stood on the surface. This must have been one of the points from which Rexin either entered or departed the area around the tower. The ground around the pit was torn apart by the large trails made by the slithering of the Divine Beast, trails that had become small streams from the pooling of rainwater.

Daniel dismounted and walked up to the edge of the pit, peering into the blackness beyond. Something in the pit smelled, an earthy and pungent odor that overpowered the smokiness of the tower. It was a stronger smell than any simple hole in the ground ought to be. The Paladin slowly lowered himself to his knees, gripping the edges of the pit, looking for anything that would help him discover which direction the creature had gone. He strained his eyes, trying desperately to discern which way the tunnel turned.

A sound beside him caused him to start, nearly toppling him into the shadowed recess. Beside him Rooker began urinating into the void, laughing as soon as he realized how much he had startled his commander. When he was done shaking the last few drops free, the drunken Paladin buttoned himself back up and took another swig of ale, then poured another gulp into the pit as he looked around at what had been his old post. Daniel thought he almost looked remorseful as he did so.

"See anything worth following?" Rooker asked between gulps.

"Not yet," Daniel replied. "Springjack! Come see this."

The mute Paladin ambled over, leaving his own horse to mill about uneasily with the others. When Springjack reached Daniel's side, he crouched beside him, looking into the earth where Daniel pointed.

"Which way did it go?" Daniel asked.

Springjack merely shrugged.

Rooker snorted. "It don't work that way, Daniel. As far as I'm concerned, it don't even work any better than me knowing what time I'm gonna shit tomorrow. All I know is that I'm gonna shit."

"Eloquent as always," Bast said, walking up. "Trust us when we say that Springjack has the sight. It will come to him, just give it time."

Daniel stood and turned, surveying the rest of the wreckage. Behind them the others were picking at garbage along the walls, looking for any personal trinkets that might have been left behind the last time they were here. Fiora and Asmov both wandered around the remains of the tower, careful to avoid any lingering hotspots from the fires.

Thinking that the entire venture here was a failure, Daniel slowly walked through the stream that separated them, the muddy water splashing across his boots.

What a mistake.

When he reached the others, Fiora simply nodded and walked past him, making a straight line for Springjack. That meant that Daniel was alone with Asmov for the first time since the Seraph had saved him all of those months ago on the plains. The pair had barely spoken since that ordeal.

The winged warrior was still trying to ignore the Paladin's presence, but Daniel decided that he need to confront Asmov at some point, and now seemed as good a time as any.

"Why are you even here, Asmov?" he asked.

The other seemed to ignore him still, intensely interested in some charred stone of no importance. After looking over every possible facet of the stone, he turned to look at Daniel, locking eyes with him. Asmov's expression was that same baleful stare that he always cast Daniel's way, though this time it was possible that he held even more hate behind his eyes.

"I left something undone on the plains, and I don't wish to leave it undone," he said, his tone even.

"I didn't figure that you would be willing to take orders from one such as me," Daniel replied.

"I won't," he scowled. "We hunt the same creature, but we do not hunt it together. I will never serve a sinspawn such as you."

"Why even travel with us then?" Daniel asked.

"Bait."

Disgusted, Daniel turned his back on the spiteful Seraph, walking back toward the hole in the center of the ruins. It would feel good to see the last of Asmov, one way or another.

Daniel stopped and turned once more.

"You didn't have to save me."

The blackened stone flew right at his face. It was snatched out of the air at the last moment by a large, gauntleted hand.

Springjack gently sat the stone on the ground between Daniel and Asmov, staring at it oddly for a few moments. Daniel couldn't help but follow the gaze of the mute warrior to the stone as well. Something about it felt ominous to him, but he couldn't say what. When Springjack looked back at Daniel, he wore an expression of great sadness on his face. His hands reached back for his new hammer, but a look from Daniel stopped him.

He's never been worth it.

Daniel returned to the center of the ruins and began unloading his horse. He tried to push the overwhelming feeling of defeat from his mind, but he found himself unable to do so. He was in over his head, and doubted that any amount of luck would change that now.

"We sleep here tonight. In the morning we head to the east," he called out to the others.

That night when Fiora tried to join him in his bedroll under the pretense of being cold he smiled but told her perhaps another night. There would be no warmth that any man or woman could bring him now. When he rolled away from her his thoughts turned to his magical sword that he had been gifted by a god. He cradled the blade in the bedding beside him, even as he drifted off. When he finally fell asleep, he dreamt of Lio descending from the sky and taking him to the Divine Plane above. As they embraced, Aenna engulfed them in a blinding, golden light.

THE NEXT MORNING Daniel awoke to find Springjack sitting where Daniel and Asmov had spoken the day before, still staring at that blackened stone. Rubbing the sleep from his eyes,

Daniel stood and made his way across the ruins to where Springjack sat. He looked at the stone as well, the ominous feelings from yesterday having abated somewhat. Now it seemed that there was nothing about the rock that made it extraordinary. When Springjack finally noticed him, the mute warrior pointed to the south. It took several moments for Daniel to realize what he meant.

"Did you have some kind of vision?" he asked, his mouth dry.

The other Paladin nodded, pointing south again. A small breeze had picked up then, wafting the scent of the pungent odor from the hole to Daniel. Springjack could communicate to others who had known him longer with hand signs, but Daniel had yet to grasp them fully.

Fiora and Bast came upon them then, Bast nodding distantly to Daniel and signing something to Springjack. Once they had gone back and forth for a bit, with Fiora jumping in, both Paladins got visibly excited.

"Did he tell you?" Fiora asked.

"As best he could," Daniel replied. "Does he know what to look for?"

"He won't say," Bast interjected. "He just says that we must head to the south."

"At this point, that is good enough for me," Daniel answered, extending a hand to Springjack.

Once the big warrior was on his feet, Daniel patted him on the back. They led the two other Paladins back toward the others, trying to hide their excitement.

The others didn't ask any questions as they loaded their horses and began riding south rather than east. The breeze continued to bring with it the earthy smell as Daniel and his band filed out of the large opening in the wall, leaving Siltstone Tower behind for the last time.

The sun was hiding behind a wall of dark clouds, its light only filtering down to them weakly. As the day wore on, the grasslands slowly gave way to the same dusty plains that Daniel had fought the creature upon the first time. This far south of Illux, the land was arid. What had been a paradise only a generation ago was becoming a lifeless waste. Resources became more important, with sources of water separated by longer and longer stretches of nothingness. Each warrior struggled with a thirst that they could not afford to fully quench. Though the heat was bearable due to the cloud cover, they could not waste water at this stage of the hunt. As for food, they still had supplies on the horses that should last them another four days at least.

The longer they headed south the more a knot formed in Daniel's stomach as he realized that they were actually nearing their destination. It seemed that Springjack noticed it too, for the great warrior grew more and more pale the later it got. He kept close to Daniel, his eyes casting this way and that nervously. Daniel even thought that he caught Springjack wiping away tears when he looked at certain members of the little band. Bast rode up beside them and tried to sign to Springjack, but the mute Paladin simply shrugged him off and kept his gaze away from him.

It was near enough to night when it happened that Daniel didn't notice the change at first. But the horses did. Daniel had been bucked off and was halfway to the ground before he noticed what was happening. He struck the earth harder than he would have liked, but didn't feel any real damage as he probed his body. Not all of the other riders had been bucked from their horses, but all of the animals had begun to frantically whinny and thrash about. As he started to pull himself up, he felt the ground beneath him begin to shake.

How did it know where we were? Are we really that lucky?

It was when he saw Asmov jump from his horse and draw his sword that Daniel realized that the creature must have sensed another bearer of Divine Blood. It was such an immense being that he was surprised that Asmov had not done the same. Either way, it seemed that, for once, having the Seraph along was good for something. Rolling to his feet, Daniel began shouting orders.

"Spread out! When it emerges we must target its eyes. Save your energy to attack with what magic you can!"

The other Paladins who weren't already on the ground dropped from their horses and sent the beasts running to safety, hoping that somehow this would go smoothly and they could find them after. By then the darkness was absolute, and it was obvious from the tremors that Rexin the Blasted was below them.

Just as suddenly as it had started, the earth-shaking stopped.

Then the eruption of stones and dust made the black air thick, and isolated Daniel from all of his companions. He tried not to breathe in the miasma, lest he be reduced to a choking fit. Blindly, Daniel stumbled backward, away from the direction that he was sure the thing had come from, realizing very quickly that whatever plan he had thought that they had formed was a complete mistake. Flashes of blue peppered the upper reaches of the air, lighting up the silhouette of a great serpentine form. The bluish tint cast a ghastly pallor over the immense creature. The Divine Beast roared defiantly and plunged downward to its left. The screams that followed sounded like Rooker, but Daniel couldn't be sure. Whoever it was, had clearly just rejoined the High God.

As the creature swallowed a mouthful of man and earth, Daniel could just make out the shiny white orb of its dead eye, reflecting the blue of the magics that bounced off of its scaly hide. He finally drew Lio's sword from its scabbard and charged forward, launching himself at Rexin while it was still low enough for him to reach. On the other side of Rexin, Asmov was flying about, shooting blasts of blue flame at its good eye.

"Shit."

Rexin turned at the last moment, noticing the Seraph that was causing it irritation. Daniel's jump was thereby invalidated and he plastered himself on the back of its neck. He tried desperately to grip onto one of the segmented scales—and failed miserably. He fell then, tumbling through the darkness and landing on the ground in a heap. To make matters worse, his sword had landed somewhere else entirely. He spat blood and cursed his damnable luck.

Bast was there then, pulling Daniel to his feet. Once he had done so, the stalwart Paladin turned and began hammering the Divine Beast with blasts of blue energy, but the creature's back was to them, giving Bast no opening to cause any real harm. The Paladin was channeling so much of his energy into his wasted attacks that the very air around him crackled and spit with sparks, lighting up his position like a beacon. Daniel stumbled away from him, blindly groping around for Lio's sword.

It has to be around here somewhere. Lio, help me.

More cries of pain came from behind—this time from Fiora it sounded like. They were all dying because of his stupid plan to attack this thing with no real means of harming it. It only he could find that damned sword. It had to do something, it was forged in the Divine Plane after all. If he had the blade, he could stick it in Rexin's eye and kill the monster. His search became more difficult as the ground began to rumble again, and the girth of the thing squeezed out of the hole and its full length was on the surface.

He heard screaming again.

Daniel looked over his shoulder to see the slithering giant tossing a dimly illuminated figure into the air before gulping it down. The figure didn't cry out as it met its demise, either because he or she was already dead—or because he was mute. Then Rexin twisted and snuffed out the blue beacon that was Bast in the blink of an eye. Daniel tried not to retch, but his limited lunch made it onto his boots somewhere. His friends, for that is what these people finally had become, were dying—because of him.

His hand brushed the pommel of his sword. Numbly, Daniel wrapped his fingers about the hilt and lifted it above his head. He let out a yell and charged at the thing that was causing so much death. Rexin had stopped slithering now, its great split maw snapping rapidly through the air at the flying figure that attacked it from the air. It was like some cosmic joke that Asmov was still alive while the others were most likely dead. Sprinting as fast as he was able, Daniel came upon the tail of the Divine Beast and continued running. The scales were slippery, forcing him to focus more on keeping his balance than continuing his climb as quickly as he was able.

More flashes of blue lit the scene below in a ghastly tableau of blues and blacks. Most of his companions seemed to be dead. Some were half-eaten and strewn about the battlefield, while others still looked as if they had been crushed in the slithering thing's wake. He could see no signs of his closest friends:

Rooker, Fiora, Bast, or Springjack. There were still some fighters down there that stood their ground, launching magic at the creature's eyes—and failing. Its head swung rapidly about as it tried to gain hold of Asmov, clearly tired of playing games with the Seraph.

"Be still you gnat!" it boomed. "You blinded me once, but never again!"

Daniel was nearing the head now, still unnoticed by some blessed luck. He crouched low against Rexin, gripping one segmented scale and then another, holding his sword tighter still. The stench of the thing was like that of the hole at Siltstone Tower, but even more pungent. From this high in the air the darkness was even more absolute than it had been upon the ground. At last he made it to the base of its head, and he knew that he could go no further safely, not while it was swinging about in the way that it was. The blackness wheeled about him as he gripped on tighter now, hoping beyond hope that some change in fortune would give him the opportunity to make it to one of the eyes.

A final scream gave him just what he wanted. Rexin stopped flailing, the Divine Beast had seemed to pause from the shock of that scream. Daniel peered over the edge of the creature to see Asmov hanging from one wing, flailing wildly about and lancing fire where he could, but clearly weakening. The Seraph had flown too close, it seemed, and not even Rexin had expected to catch him in its jaws. Daniel took the opportunity and stood, gripping Lio's sword with both hands. Then in one motion he dropped off of the side of Rexin's head, trailing the point of his sword behind him as he did so. Rexin's eye was slit in two.

We're even now, Asmov.

Rexin roared and twisted in pain, dropping Asmov and knocking Daniel from the air. The Paladin didn't drop his sword this time, but he did fall all of the way to the earth, striking his head when he landed on something sticky and soft.

When his eyes opened again it was just as dark as it had been, and yet the creature hadn't found him. A shape passed by the edge of Daniel's vision, clutching a twisted wing to its side. Daniel pushed himself up and saw Rexin's tail disappearing into a hole in the ground. Absentmindedly, he placed his hand onto what had cushioned his fall. If he hadn't vomited earlier he surely would have then.

Ahead of Daniel, Asmov continued to limp ahead, moving slowly but determinedly from the site of the attack. It didn't look like there were any other survivors in the area, so Daniel grudgingly decided to follow Asmov, focusing what little healing energy he had at the bloody cut on his head.

The rumbling under his feet began to recede, but the darkness persisted. It seemed that Rexin wasn't done with them, even with a new injury. Belatedly, Daniel realized that he wasn't actually sure which eye he had slit open. It was very possible that the creature, while wounded, was no less blind than it had been before. Even if it was blind, that still wouldn't stop the thing. He needed to use the soft flesh of the eye to get inside the scales, which he had failed to do. That would be the only way that anything short of another Divine Beast would be able to finish this monster.

Ahead, looming above them in the darkness was a great shadow, like a small mountain that had formed out of nowhere. It seemed that this was where Asmov was headed, some last bastion of safety for the Seraph now that he was grounded just like all of the Paladins that had been devoured before him. It was another few minutes before the rumbling slowly returned, Rexin apparently deciding to finish them both. By then, Asmov had already begun to pull himself up the shadowy edifice and away from the dangers below. Daniel reached it moments later, following the Seraph handhold after handhold, his fingers gripping the hard stone ladder that was leading him to freedom.

By the time Rexin emerged to the surface, both men were panting on the top of a large blackened stone.

5

How many hours had they been trapped up there together? The lack of any stars, or even an indication that it was still night at all in the world outside of the nightmare that they found themselves trapped in, made it impossible to tell. For the first four hours they had each laid there, panting, coughing, and even crying. Neither had spoken to or attempted to heal the other, both isolated in every way imaginable. Below, Rexin raged against the stone, smashing its teeth and head into the edifice in a vain attempt to collapse the bastion of safety that its prey had found. So far it had been unsuccessful in its efforts, but the thing would not give up on the mortals who had robbed it of its vision and evaded it three times.

Is this punishment for my birth? Is this what end I have earned?

Rexin slithered around the great stone and rested, apparently tiring from its exertions. Daniel audibly sighed in relief. He was no longer light-headed, his wound finally healed from what little energy he was able to spare. Still, the back of his head was caked with blood from both himself and the body that had cushioned his fall.

As for Asmov and his wing, Daniel wasn't sure. All that he knew was that the Seraph lay just feet from him, still drawing some scattered, ragged breaths. Neither of them seemed to want to be the first one to break the silence, almost as if that would rob them of what little safety they had left. Daniel truly didn't mind. Asmov had hated him from the first, never forgiving him for the nature of his conception. He wasn't alone in that hatred, but the extreme nature of it was singular to just Asmov. Not many had ever been able to overlook what Daniel was but a select few, some of whom were fighting up north, while the rest were either dead or dying here in the south. With his friends so few and far between it seemed fitting that he was fated to die beside his most hated foe.

Daniel's tongue felt like sand as it ran across his lips. They had no food or water with them up here, no supplies to last them the weeks that the Divine Beast would surely be willing to wait to kill its tormentors. He wished that he hadn't left his water skin with his horse—not that it would have survived the fall from Rexin in any case. Daniel loosely gripped Lio's sword in his right hand. Why had he thought so much of this weapon? It was clearly not of this world, yet in the hands of a mortal it was no different than any other steel. He had allowed his fascination with the God of Light to cloud his judgment. He had allowed his anger with Asmov to cloud his judgment. He had allowed his desire to make himself loved cloud his judgment. After all, wasn't that why he was dying up here? Wasn't that why he had thrown away all of the lives of his friends?

He must have been ruminating on his misfortune for

longer than he had realized. The slithering of the Divine Beast below stirred him from his thoughts. Daniel noticed the same stench of the creature again, possibly for the first time since he had been stranded on the rock. He rolled onto his side and pulled himself to the edge of the rock and leaned over. What little he could make out was that Rexin was restless again, lifting as high as it could and striking at his position like an adder. Every blow came up short of where he lay by several dozen yards, the creature angrily splitting its jaws and hissing in distaste.

"Curse you, cowards!" Rexin thundered. "I will devour your bones. I will crush you beneath my path! You think that blinding me will stop me?"

Daniel spat over the ledge and made obscene gestures that we was sure the creature wouldn't understand. When he was done, Daniel crawled back from the ledge and found Asmov sitting upright and watching him. From what Daniel could see, it seemed that the Seraph's wing was still bent at an odd angle. There was no light to reflect in Asmov's steely eyes, but Daniel could guess what his expression was.

"What is your great plan now?" Asmov rasped.

"I plan on dying at some point today," Daniel laughed.

The Seraph was quiet for a moment, looking out into the darkness beyond the edge of the rock. He finally turned and stared back at Daniel again.

"This was a fool's errand from the beginning. We should have had a whole battalion of Seraphs, and a Divine Beast of our own," he spat. "Why would Lio have allowed this?"

"Have you communed with him?" Daniel asked.

"No," Asmov answered. "It is not his blood that I share. I was made of Luna. She knows some of what we experience, but her focus is on that battles in the north. The gods will not worry about two men dying in the south."

All Seraphs shared the Divine Blood of the gods. Whichever god had created them with his or her blood could speak to them from then on, no matter how much distance separated them. It seemed that such powers would do little to help them now, not with more pressing matters taking the attention of the gods elsewhere.

"Well then, I say we take one final strike at its eyes. If we can get past the eye to the soft flesh behind, we can kill it," Daniel said.

Asmov spat again. "I'll admit that you don't give up, do you, sinspawn?"

Daniel lunged at him then, but the Seraph just batted him away and laughed again.

"Please don't mind me, I couldn't help myself," Asmov continued. "I bet you never thought that you would die by my side."

Nor did you.

Daniel ignored him and looked back over the edge. Rexin had stopped lashing at the side of the rock and had begun tunneling back under the ground. He heard this change in the creatures behavior, rather than saw it. The perpetual darkness still did not lift, so he knew that the Divine Beast was not going far. Perhaps, it had simply tired of attacking them in vain, or maybe it could only be above ground for a certain period of time. It was possible that it was going to attempt to bring down the blackened stone from below, sealing the fate of the two men for sure.

"Do you ever feel like a pawn, Daniel?" Asmov broke the silence again.

"What?" Daniel sounded incredulous as he turned around.

"We serve and fight for our gods, we kill and die for them," the Seraph said. "But what about us? What about our choices? Would you be here if it wasn't for the gods?"

Daniel clutched Lio's sword tighter.

"I would. It was my decision to come here. I led those people here to their deaths," Daniel answered. "That was no god."

"That is why I saved you on the plain," Asmov whispered. "I never liked you, sinspawn, but out there I respected you. Fate, the gods, they chose a life for you when your bastard father raped your mother, but you spat in their face."

"If you respected me so much, then why do you hate me so much? How can you do both?"

"Unlike you, I had no choice," Asmov's voice faltered at the end.

Daniel looked away from him, more confused by the sudden crack in the other man's hateful exterior than emotionally affected. Daniel had seen men waiver in their lifelong convictions just before the end, for he had seen more than one veteran die bleeding out in the muck. But a man like Asmov? That he did not expect. How honest was the Seraph being, in any case?

"We can't do anything until Rexin comes back to the surface," Daniel said. "And I don't foresee that happening without us giving it some incentive."

"You mean bait?" Asmov whispered.

"Yes. You suggested it before."

All was silent again, longer this time than it had been in a while. There were no animals that Daniel could here, nor was there any breeze. It was as silent as a battlefield before the crows arrived. The smell of Rexin wafted back to his nostrils, turning Daniel's thoughts to what he must do.

It's the only way to end this.

"Which one of us?" Asmov asked, sullenly.

"It must be me," Daniel said quietly. "Only the strength of a Seraph can hope to overcome this thing. I will give you Lio's blade to do the deed."

"How will you do it?"

"I've thought about it. I can't jump from here, the fall may kill me," Daniel said. "I will need to climb down. We need it to think that I am running for safety, we need it to hear me through the earth."

"It won't work," the Seraph rasped, slowly standing and walking toward the edge, peering off. "I barely have the strength to stand, let alone kill that thing."

It's the only way.

"What do you suggest then?" Daniel asked, turning his back to the other.

"I don't. You are right that only a Seraph will be able to finish the beast; you certainly never could. Perhaps if we wait another few hours I can do something. I don't know."

Daniel walked the small perimeter of the rock that they stood on, carefully feeling his way around the edge with his feet. When he could he peered over the edge, seeing nothing below them but unending darkness. They were running out of options, it seemed, and Daniel knew it. They didn't have time to wait a few more hours, even if it was possible that they would last that long. Even if they did last, the lack of food or water would surely sap the other warrior's strength, not add to it. With no strength to heal himself, Asmov would never stand a chance.

The Paladin looked down at the sword clutched in his hand. In the darkness it almost looked black to him. He looked back at Asmov, hoping to find some kind of answer there. The outline of the Seraph was all that was visible, allowing Daniel to fill in the details between the lines. The Seraph still looked into the void, keeping whatever thoughts he had to himself. Even with the lack of light, Daniel could make out the crooked angle of one of his wings, still not truly healed. There was no way that Asmov would be able to kill that thing alone. Maybe they could work together somehow? Wouldn't that be poetic in some way? But Daniel knew that wouldn't work.

There was no getting past what he needed to do.

Asmov sighed and leaned forward, looking back over the edge farther than he had leaned yet.

"Do you think there is a chance we could make it back to the city?" Asmov muttered, more to himself than to Daniel. "You may be ready to die, sinspawn, but I am not."

"If we try to run we would both die as cowards, rather than one of us a hero," Daniel responded.

It's the only way.

"Alright. I'll do it," the Seraph sighed again. "I just want to know one thing before its over."

Daniel slowly approached the same ledge that Asmov gazed out over, still clutching the sword before him. He could smell that pungent odor of the Divine Beast again, and for once it didn't seem out of place. He had thought that he was ready for this moment, but there would never be a way to truly be ready for death. Not a death like he was about to face.

"What is that?" he asked, finally, his mouth parched.

"Will you forgive me? Not just for this, but for everything?" It sounded like Asmov was crying. "You are one of the bravest men that I have ever met. I've never liked you, I still don't. But gods, you are braver than I."

No, I'm not.

"Yes," Daniel whispered. "I forgive you. Will you forgive me?"

The sword that Lio gave him lashed out, hacking Asmov's good wing at the base, nearly severing it. Warm blood splattered across Daniel's face. The Seraph shrieked like an animal, more from shock than from pain. Daniel closed his mind to the sounds, grateful that the darkness masked the most heinous details of the sight before him. The Paladin struck again, taking Asmov in the hip this time, his blade biting deep and reaching bone. When he pulled the blade free, Daniel planted his boot in the Seraph's back and sent him careening wildly over the edge, falling to what would soon be his death. Asmov spun, end over end, crying out during the entire fall. The sounds that escaped the dying man's lips were unintelligible. Daniel could see him no longer, but he did hear the crunch as the Seraph hit the earth far below. It seemed that the fall had not been a quick death, for the man now moaned weakly.

The rumble that greeted the Seraph's collision could not be felt by Daniel high atop the stone, but he could sense it. Within moments the earth erupted again as Rexin raised itself from the stony depths with such force that dust and stones showered Daniel even high above where he stood. What happened to Asmov he couldn't tell but the distant moaning either stopped or was drown out by the sound of the Divine Beast returning to the surface.

Swinging its head about in a sweeping motion, Rexin's eye landed upon the location where Daniel crouched. Daniel peppered the air around the beast with bursts of magic, illuminating Rexin just enough that he could see the eye. The Paladin sprung, arcing through the air at the cavity where one of the orbs would be. Even with the limited light from his magic, he could only see the vaguest outline of the thing he aimed for, hoping beyond hope that he wasn't going to plant himself into a squamous patch of flesh. When he neared the Divine Beast, Daniel swung his sword from high above his head, splitting through the soft flesh of its eye. The membrane gave way under the edge of his blade, allowing his entire body to enter the gelatinous mass. The fluid passed in and around him, filling his eyes and ears and nostrils with the thick goop. Daniel held his breath, ignoring the stink and the taste of it, thinking only of those who had died.

Those who I have killed.

He raised the sword again and again, cutting deeper and deeper into the soft flesh. Worse even than the smells was the sound of the soft flesh parting before him. The world around Daniel became wet and hot as what he knew was silver and black blood gushed over him. Outside, Rexin thrashed and swung its head about, but the Paladin had gotten too deep to be shaken free. Finally, he breeched the softer areas and reached something thicker. It was then that Daniel stopped cutting and began blasting wildly with blue energy. From what little that his eyes could make out during the flashes of light, it looked as if he had reached the creature's brain.

With his lungs screaming in pain, Daniel finally took several massive gulps, filling his mouth with all manner of fluids. Then he felt the world drop out from under him as Rexin slumped and rushed toward the ground below. Daniel felt the shift in the world around him. He stabbed his sword as deep into the harder flesh as he could and held on for dear life. When the impact finally arrived he wasn't shaken about as much as he had anticipated, but his head did strike against a piece of solid bone.

Dazed, the Paladin thought that he saw a glimmer of light above him, but there was no way that could be possible.

Eventually, he pulled his sword free and began climbing toward the light, occasionally stopping to wipe the blood and gore from his face and eyes. For the first time since this battle had begun, he was grateful that his stomach was empty. After several slow-going moments of climbing out of the eye socket of the Divine Beast, Daniel collapsed onto the side of Rexin the Blasted, lying there, alone, in the sunlight.

He wasn't sure how long he had been lying there when they came. At first he had thought them illusions, the fabrications of an addled mind. After all, the three figures who approached him out of the blinding light were all dead. Daniel had heard each one of them as they had been devoured by Rexin the Blasted the night before. He was sure of it.

"You've got to be shittin' me," Rooker coughed, covering his nose. "You took this thing down by yourself?"

"Rooker!" Fiora shouted, kneeling next to Daniel and examining him.

The Paladin was lying on the ground now, somehow having dragged himself off of the great carcass and falling onto the dirt below. A pool of black and silver blood had flowed out the creature, creating a moat that rounded the fallen warrior. He blinked in confusion at the ghost who kneeled over him, a warmth flowing from her fingers into his body. Some bones had been broken; he was sure of that once he noticed the pain. The warmth was knitting him back together piece by piece, and slowly giving him his mental faculties back as well.

When she was done, Fiora stepped away and nodded to

Springjack, who knelt and picked Daniel up, cradling him against his body. The mute warrior carried him away from the stinking carcass of the Divine Beast and whatever secrets lay hidden in its gullet. It was when the body of the thing was receding in the distance that Daniel looked down at the sword clutched tightly in his grip. Its blade, though no longer wet with blood, had turned completely black.

6

Springjack eyed the black blade uneasily, never letting it out of his sight.

Does he know?

For the third time in as many months, Daniel walked through the gates to Illux after an encounter with Rexin the Blasted in the wilderness beyond. For the first time he walked back through those gates victorious, for he had killed the beast and ridden the world of its presence. Even so, he felt hollow. Of his little band that had ridden out of the city over a week before, now only three beside himself remained: Rooker, Fiora and Springjack. Those three had not been killed by Rexin during the final attack as he had thought, but instead they had fled the area until the darkness had ended, pulled to safety by the mute warrior, it seemed. Bast and the others had not been so fortunate. Rexin had slaughtered each and every one of them. When the night was finally lifted, the surviving three had journeyed back to the site of the battle, where they had found Daniel at the corpse of the giant snake.

None of them had asked what had happened to Asmov, and Daniel had not spoken of it. Nor would he, ever. Without his sacrifice, Rexin would never have been defeated, and who knows how many other lives would have ended from its reign of terror? Asmov would have understood. What had happened needed to have happened. Rexin had to have been killed.

But at what cost?

Daniel looked down at Lio's sword now, held out before him because he was unwilling to put it back into its scabbard. Its surface was like onyx now, and no matter how many times he cleaned it, it would not change back to its original silver. He told himself that it had turned black from all of Rexin's blood, the sickly liquid somehow getting absorbed by the heavenly metal.

Yet in his heart he knew that it was red blood that had stained it, not black.

The fanfare when they had returned was limited, to say the least. Tyga had ridden out to meet them again, leading them back slowly and keeping a close eye on Springjack. Her interactions with the mute warrior gave Daniel the first smile that he had allowed himself to have since Rexin had been felled. If anything good had come of this, other than the death of that beast, he had finally found himself with more than a single friend. With any luck, the four of them would be able to join the fighting in the Rim after whatever came next.

I hope they get along with Merek, I have so few friends, after all. Will he even believe what I have done?

As they walked through the streets of Illux, now slightly more crowded than they had been when the party had left, a small crowd began to gather behind the returning heroes, wondering what news they would have for Lio. None of the other gods had returned from the north yet, though some of the fighters had come back to gain some respite between the major battles of the campaign. Many of these followed the group now, having heard that some brave warriors had gone out and killed a Divine Beast with little heavenly aid. Daniel tried to keep an eye out for his friend Merek, but he never saw him.

Ahead, the cathedral loomed above again, just as it had before everything had changed. The knife in Daniel's stomach twisted, his fear of what was to come outweighed only by his desire to see Lio again. The one thing that had kept him from losing himself on the long walk back to Illux were thoughts of the golden face and white hair of the god. Lio stood on the steps of the cathedral again, surrounded by a large crowd of onlookers. He appeared to be eagerly awaiting the returning band.

When they were close, Lio called out. "What news?"

Those around Daniel respectfully stayed silent, allowing him to answer when he was ready. He wasn't. The Paladin did the unthinkable and refused the question of the god, instead slowly trudging through the mass of onlookers and up the steps to be closer to Lio, just one more time. The now-familiar warmth of being near the god washed over him. When he finally opened his mouth it was dry and his tongue stuck to the roof of it. Taking a deep breath to steady himself, he finally spoke.

"Rexin the Blasted is dead!" he called out, raising Lio's sword above his head.

The crowd began shouting and cheering, their exuberance drowning out even Daniel's discomfort. They were cheering for *him*. He tried to bury his misgivings behind false bravado, and it felt good. From within the audience a chant erupted, quiet at first, but quickly taking over any of the other sounds in the plaza.

"Nightbreaker!" they chanted. "Nightbreaker!"

Beside Daniel, Rooker and Fiora took up the chant as well. After a few minutes, Lio took the cry up also, his voice drowning out all of the others. Daniel looked up at him and saw the god beaming.

Some time later, after his audience had gone back to their regular comings and goings, Daniel was left alone with Lio in the plaza. Rooker and Fiora had gone into the city to find a tavern somewhere to get drunk. Springjack had hung around the longest, but had taken his final leave when none were left but Lio and Daniel.

But it had seemed to Daniel that the two had been alone together from the moment that the chanting had stopped.

The Paladin looked down at his sword again. Its black blade glinted in the final rays of the sun. Lio looked at him with an odd expression, almost one of longing. Daniel stared back at him until he became so uncomfortable that his eyes fell back to the sword.

His blade.

Daniel suddenly fell to one knee and held the sword up above his head, returning it to the god who had graced him with such a powerful gift. It felt heavy on the palms of his hands, and suddenly holding it up became a chore. Lio lifted the sword from Daniel's outstretched hands and examined it, staring intently at the onyx surface before returning it to Daniel.

"Keep it," the god said, smiling. "It is yours now. My gift to you."

Daniel gripped the blade tightly and returned it to his side before slowly standing. He was relieved that Lio had not commented on the discoloration of his old weapon. The Paladin sheathed the steel and looked at his feet, hoping to find an opportunity to retire for the night.

"What will you name it?" Lio asked after another silence. "All great things should have a name. The people have named you Nightbreaker, but what of your sword?"

"I would rather the sword bear the name than I," Daniel replied. "It was the sword that shed the blood, not me."

"It is settled then. The Champion Daniel and his blade, Nightbreaker. Songs will be sung of your exploits, of that I have no doubt."

Daniel finally looked away from his feet and gazed at Lio again, the god seemingly glowing more than he had been all the while that they had spoken. It was then that all of his guilt and fear faded. He felt a lone tear run down his cheek—the last that he would cry for Asmov. Rexin the Blasted was dead, and Daniel had done the deed. Daniel, who had been born of sin, had killed the Divine Beast and earned the respect of a god. He was no longer just a sinspawn. He would never be seen the same way again, by himself or those around him.

"You will do great things," the god said, leaning in. "This I know."

Without thinking, Daniel reached out and grabbed Lio by the hand, pulling him in close—and kissing him on the mouth. Whatever happened next he didn't notice, for a god kissed him back.

WHAT TO READ NEXT

To follow the adventures of Daniel, read *The Northern Campaign,* currently on our Patreon and coming soon to print.

To see the state of the world some thousand years after Daniel became a legend, check out *Wrath of the Fallen.*

ABOUT THE AUTHOR

Kris Jerome was born in the middle of a snowstorm in Pendleton, Oregon, several decades ago. Since then he moved the great distance across the state to study at Willamette University. He obtained a BFA in Digital Communication Arts in June of 2016 from Oregon State University. Kris enjoys reading books and comics while sipping wine and craft beer. He currently lives in Albany, Oregon with his wife, seven children and two cats.

darktidingspress.com
darktidingspress@gmail.com

www.ingramcontent.com/pod-product-compliance
Lightning Source LLC
Chambersburg PA
CBHW021957040826
48979CB00044B/1892/J
9781951138202